MW00946139

Lilly and Madi's Playtime Dilemma

Nancy J. Yakopovich

Illustrations by José Antonio Acosta Pérez

Lilly and Madi's Playtime Dilemma

ISBN 978-9945-637-16-8

©**Nancy J. Yakopovich, 2023**
For this edition:
©**Editorial Isla Negra, 2023**

It is prohibited to reproduce in total or in part this book without the express consent of the author and the publisher.

Images in cover and interiors
José Antonio Acosta Pérez
Design of cover and interiors
Iván Figueroa Luciano
Publishing house reader
Doris E. Lugo Ramírez, Ph.D.
Final correction
Alexis X. Bruno Mendoza

Editorial Isla Negra
P. O. Box 364991
San Juan, Puerto Rico 00936-4991
www.islanegra.com

Distributed in USA by
Peach Hollow Publications
peachhollowpubs@gmail.com

Printed in the United States of America

DEDICATION

To my children, Kyle, Katie, Jake and Jimmy, and to all of my grandchildren. You are the love that overflows inside of me. You are my inspiration. You are my life.

Love,
Mom/Grammy

ACKNOWLEDGMENTS

I would like to thank my husband, John, my children, my family, and my friends for their continued support and encouragement. I rely on you tremendously, and you never fail to be there for me.

To Jose Antonio Acosta Pérez, my illustrator… thank you for the beautiful, artistic designs you created for Lilly and Madi's Playtime Dilemma.

To Marcela Gómez Lugo… thank you for your translating expertise and support!

To my friend, Doris E. Lugo Ramírez, Ph.D.… thank you for your editing skills and continued words of encouragement.

To Ivan Figueroa Luciano… thank you for your talents and the brilliant design layout you created!

To my Public Relations and Marketing Coordinator, Yvonne L. Eaglehouse, Ph.D.… thank you for your advice, technical support, and marketing prowess!

To my beta readers… thank you for leading me in the right direction.

And finally, a special thank you to my publisher, Carlos R. Gomez Beras. It was his validation of my writing skills that pushed me to move outside of my box and attain the dream I have had since I was a child. Many hugs and blessings to you.

Lilly and Madi were cousins.

But they weren't *just* cousins, they were best friends and they loved playing together.

They skipped rope together.

They played hopscotch together.

On their swings they sat together, side by side,

and soared as high as they could go!

They blew bubbles together and laughed

8

when the bubbles popped on their noses.

And they loved walking to the little store
just around the corner to buy pieces of candy
that they could share.

But there was one thing they did NOT like doing together. And this annoyed them because...

Lilly loved llamas,

and Madi loved sloths!

Lilly liked pretending she was a llama. She trotted through the yard and up and down the sidewalk just like a llama. And she made snorting noises as she ran around Madi over and over again. Lilly the Llama liked climbing over hills and stretching her tall neck to peer all about.

"C'mon, Madi, climb the hill with me," Lilly the Llama called out. "C'mon Madi, catch up to me! You are too slow," Lilly the Llama said in frustration. It annoyed Lilly when her cousin dillydallied so far behind.

But Madi, who liked pretending she was a sloth, took her good old time. Because, after all, sloths moved very slowly.

"I can't catch up," Madi the Sloth said in her slowest of slow voices. "I...aaammm aaa slooothhh!"

Madi put one foot out, very slowly, and then the other. And then she did it again in her slowest of slow motions. Madi the Sloth blinked her eyes and turned her head very slowly from side to side before moving on.

It annoyed Madi when her cousin ran ahead of her, and especially when Lilly bounced around her in circles.

Both of them, now annoyed
and frustrated, decided to go home.

23

Lilly went to her father complaining, "Madi is too slow! She likes being a sloth but I'm too fast for her! I don't know why she wants to be a sloth anyhow!" Lilly crossed her arms and grumbled as she squeezed her furry llama doll.

"Well, why don't you try being a sloth the next time you play with Madi," her father told her. "You might even like being a sloth!" So Lilly the Llama gave that some thought.

At the same time, Madi went to her mother and complained, "I don't like playing with Lilly when she's a llama! She's too fast and she makes me dizzy when she runs around me in circles!" Madi continued to grumble as she slid down to the floor in her cozy sloth slippers.

"Well, why don't you try being a llama the next time you play with Lilly," said her mother. "You might even like being a llama!" So Madi the Sloth gave that some thought.

When the two cousins got together again, Madi surprised Lilly by saying, "Let's play llama this morning!"

Lilly's smile grew wide and she jumped with glee, in llama fashion of course.

"OK, Madi! And this afternoon we'll play sloth!"

Madi yelled, "Yiipppeee!" in sloth mode of course.

As it turned out, the morning was cool. The two llamas were full of energy as they trotted up hills and over trails of pebbles and twigs. They carried packs on their backs as they navigated through mountains that they made with empty boxes stacked high. By noon time, Lilly the Llama and Madi the Llama were tired. They spent a busy morning playing and acting as llamas do.

The afternoon grew warm. So the two cousins loosened their packs and dropped to their hands and knees. Lazily they crawled to the nearest shade tree and rolled in the cool, soft grass. They giggled and laughed as they spoke verrry slowwwly. They stretched and yawned and munched on pretzel sticks. Because you know, sloths like eating sticks!

Once they finished munching, Madi the Sloth and Lilly the Sloth slowwwly walked to the swing set, putting one foot forward and then the other. They climbed on its bars as though it was a tree, blinked their eyes and slowly turned their heads from side to side. They spent a busy afternoon playing and acting as sloths do.

Make a drawing of Lilly and Madi playing like sloths in the tree.

Before they knew it
the afternoon ended

32

and it was time now for the
two cousins to go home.

What a wonderful day they had!

Both couldn't wait to tell their

parents how they played together

as Llama-Llama, Sloth-Sloth!

Tucked into bed wearing her llama pajamas and squeezing her furry llama doll, Lilly told her father, "You were right, I liked being a sloth!"

Kissing her goodnight her father replied,
"That's good to hear! Good night, Lilly the Sloth."

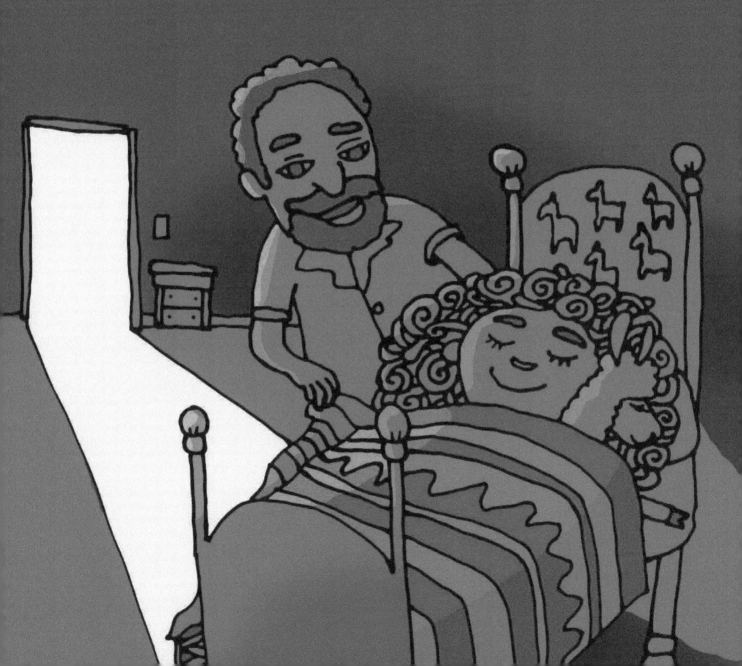

And tucked into her bed still wearing her cozy sloth slippers and cuddling her soft sloth doll, Madi told her mother, "You were right, I liked being a llama!"

Kissing her goodnight her mother replied, "That's good to hear! Good night, Madi the Llama."

Printed in the USA
CPSIA information can be obtained
at www.ICGtesting.com
LVHW062139211123
764266LV00034B/2